The Berenstain Bears
GET THE GIMMIES

When a cub's behavior
takes a turn for the worst,
it's hard for parents
to know what to do first.

A First Time Book®

The Berenstain Bears
GET THE GIMMIES

Stan & Jan Berenstain

Random House 🏠 New York

Library of Congress Cataloging-in-Publication Data:
Berenstain, Stan. The Berenstain bears get the gimmies. (A First time book)
SUMMARY: Gran and Gramps come up with a plan to help selfish Brother and Sister Bear get rid of a bad case of the galloping greedy gimmies. [1. Selfishness—Fiction. 2. Behavior—Fiction. 3. Bears—Fiction] I. Berenstain, Jan. II. Title.
III. Series: Berenstain, Stan. First time books. PZ7.B4483Beoh 1988 [E]
88-42587 ISBN: 0-394-80566-6 (pbk.); 0-394-90566-0 (lib. bdg.)

Manufactured in the United States of America 4 5 6 7 8 9 0

Of course, the members of the Bear family, who lived in the big tree house down a sunny dirt road in Bear Country, loved each other. They loved each other very much. Brother and Sister Bear loved their mama and papa. Naturally, Mama and Papa Bear loved their cubs, and, of course, they were nice to them— as nice as they could be.

But sometimes, *sometimes* they were a little too nice. Sometimes the cubs got too many treats, too many toys, and too many rides on the Bucking Duck at the mall.

Maybe that's why Brother and Sister Bear got the gimmies. Or maybe it was because there were treats, toys, and fun things to do wherever they looked—at the supermarket, at the mall, on TV, and just about every which-where.

Maybe that was why they began making a fuss
to get what they wanted—especially at the
supermarket checkout, where there were always
stacks and stacks of candy and other goodies.

"Now, cubs," Mama Bear said as the family
got into the checkout line and she saw that old
gimmie gleam in their eyes, "we can't have a big
fuss every time we pass candy. I simply won't
stand for it."

"But, Mama," whined Sister. "They have Gummy Gumballs! My favorite!"

"And Chewy Chompers! *My* favorite!" whined Brother.

"Now, hush!" said Mama. "I simply won't listen to another word..."

That's when Papa Bear smiled and said, "Now, Mama, you're only young once," and handed the cubs their favorite treats.

"It's only too true," said Mama as they were
leaving the supermarket, "that you're only young
once. But that's all the more reason to learn
proper behavior while you're still young, and I
certainly think—"

"Look! Look!" shouted Sister. "A new ride!"

"Hey, a Bucking Frog!" shouted Brother. "That
looks even better than the Bucking Duck! May we
ride it, please? May we? May we? Please!"

Now, Papa had just bought them treats, and he thought that was enough for one day. But the cubs made such a fuss that he sighed, dug into his pocket, and put some money in the slot.

Papa looked at Mama and shrugged. "Cubs will be cubs," he said.

"It may be true that cubs will be cubs," said Mama as they walked across the parking lot to their car. "But that's no excuse for jumping up and down and making a scene every time they see something they want—"

"Look! Look!" shouted the cubs once again. "Little rubber cats that stick out their tongues when you squeeze them!"

"Cubs," said Mama, "that will be quite enough! I don't want to hear another word..."

"Oh please!" they shouted. "May we have them? Please! Please! Please!" Papa decided it was time to put a stop to all the fussing.

"Stop that fussing!" he said in his loudest Papa Bear voice. But they were making such a commotion they didn't even hear him. Sister was jumping up and down so hard that she fell over backward and started kicking her feet in the air.

"Please! Please!" shouted the cubs so loudly that the whole parking lot took notice.

"Er—" said embarrassed Papa to the toy seller, "two of those rubber pussycats, please."

The rubber pussycats not
only stuck out their tongues
when you squeezed them, they
went squeak-squeak as well.
And they squeak-squeaked
all the way home.

Mama was quite annoyed by the time they got back to the tree house, but Papa was so angry he could hardly speak. It wasn't until the cubs had gone about their business and Mama had made a pot of tea that Papa's voice came back loud and clear.

"Of all the outrageous, disgraceful, *embarrassing* behavior I have ever seen," he roared, "that selfish, greedy performance by our cubs was the worst! Brother and Sister have the worst case of the galloping greedy gimmies I've ever seen!"

"Yes," said Mama, calmly sipping her tea. "But have you ever stopped to think about *why* they have the gimmies? Perhaps their greedy behavior isn't all their fault. Perhaps it's partly our fault for giving in every time they make a fuss."

Papa listened quietly. "Perhaps so," he said.

"It's up to us," she continued, "to explain things to them—to help them understand why it's important not to be greedy."

Then Papa called the cubs in for a talking-to.
He told them why it wasn't a good idea to be
selfish and greedy and want everything in sight.
  "Selfish, greedy cubs," he explained,
"can never be happy, because you just
can't have everything you want all
the time—life isn't like
that. Do you understand?"
  "Oh yes, Papa. We
understand," they said.

He talked to them about "counting their blessings," which meant enjoying the things they had instead of forever wanting more and more and more.

"Does that make sense to you?" he asked.

"Oh yes, Papa," they said. "It makes a lot of sense."

That's when the cubs heard the sound of a familiar car door. It was Grizzly Gramps and Gran come to call.

Brother and Sister ran to open the front door, and as Gramps and Gran came up the steps, they made the biggest fuss yet.

"Whaja-bringme?" they screamed. "Whaja-bringme? Whaja-bringme?!" That did it.

"Up to your room!" roared Papa. "Up to your room and no TV or treats for a week! For a *month*! For a *year*!"

The cubs knew this wasn't the time to argue. They scurried up the stairs and into their room.

"We seem to have come at a bad time!" said Gran.
"What about these things we brought with us?" asked
Gramps. "A puzzle for Brother and a top for Sister?"
"Your presents will have to wait, Gramps,"
answered Mama. "I'm afraid Brother and Sister
have a bad case of the gimmies."
"The *galloping greedy* gimmies,"
added Papa. "The worst case I've
ever seen."

The cubs opened their
door a crack to listen.

"The worst case, ya say?" said Gramps, looking Papa in the eye. "Seems to me you were quite a gimmie-cub yourself when you were little."

Brother and Sister sneaked to the top of the stairs so they could hear better.

"I was?" said Papa.

RUFE GRIZZLY'S
GENERAL
STORE

"Of course, we didn't have malls or supermarkets back then. But there was old Rufe Grizzly's General Store. Wonderful place. Sold just about everything— honey cake, licorice sticks, molasses apples, and all sorts of toys and novelties. And did you ever have the gimmies! Did you ever! You wanted everything in sight. Downright embarrassing. Why, it got so bad we couldn't go there anymore."

"So we worked out a deal," said Gran. "When it came time for a trip to the General Store, we had you decide on a treat ahead of time. It could be a sweet, a toy, or a book—and that was it for the day."

"Right," said Gramps. "And if you came down with the gimmies, we went right home and you got *nothing*!"

"That sounds like a pretty good plan to me," said Mama.

"Me too," said Papa.

The cubs tiptoed back to their room. It sounded okay to them, too.

The next time the Bear family went to the supermarket, they tried the Gramps-and-Gran plan. And it worked!

Brother decided he would get a book about dinosaurs, and Sister wanted a new box of crayons.

Mama and Papa were very proud when the cubs passed the candy rack without so much as a peep. Brother and Sister were pretty proud of themselves, too.

But then they heard it: the familiar sound of a cub with a bad case of the gimmies. The kicking, screaming cub was just behind them in the checkout line. You never *heard* such a fuss.

"What outrageous, disgraceful, embarrassing behavior!" said Sister. *"May we leave?"*

"Yeah," said Brother. "Let's get out of here."

And that's how Brother and Sister
Bear got rid of a pretty bad case
of the galloping greedy gimmies.